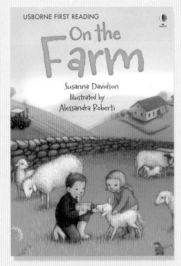

USBORNE FIRST READING

On the Farm

Susanna Davidson

Illustrated by
Alessandra Roberti

USBORNE FIRST READING

The Three Wishes

Retold by Lesley Sims
Illustrated by Elisa Squillace

14

USBORNE FIRST READING

The Sun and the Wind

Retold by
Mairi Mackinnon
Illustrated by Francesca di Chiara

USBORNE FIRST READING

The Rabbit's Tale

Retold by Lynne Benton
Illustrated by Fred Blunt

Anansi and the Tug of War

Retold by Lesley Sims
Illustrated by Alida Massari

Reading consultant: Alison Kelly
Roehampton University

Lancashire Library Services	
30118125112411	
PETERS	JF
£4.99	17-Oct-2012

Anansi was king
of the spiders.

One day, he saw
Elephant.

"Hello little Anansi,"
said Elephant.

"Little?" said Anansi.
"I'm not little.

I'm a king!
And I'm stronger
than you."

Elephant laughed.

"I'll show you,"
said Anansi.

"Let's have a tug of war."

He found a long vine

and gave one end
to Elephant.

"Start to pull when I tug it," said Anansi.

He ran through
the jungle.

Soon, he saw Rhino.

"Do you want a tug of
war?" Anansi asked.

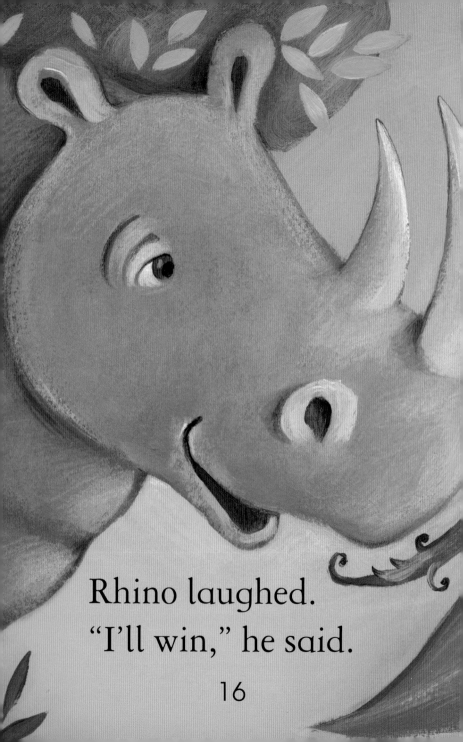

Rhino laughed.
"I'll win," he said.

Anansi gave him the other end of the vine.

"Start to pull when I tug it," said Anansi.

He ran off.

Anansi tugged
on the vine.

Elephant pulled.

Rhino pulled.

They pulled
and pulled.

At last, they were too
tired to pull any more.

Anansi ran back
to Elephant.

Elephant *was* surprised.

PUZZLES

Puzzle 1

Can you spot the differences
between these two pictures?

There are six to find.

Puzzle 2
Fill in the missing word.

vine   king

laughed   surprised

Anansi was _____ of the spiders.

Rhino _____.

Anansi tugged the _____.

Elephant *was* _____.

Puzzle 3
Can you match the word to the picture?

eating   pulling

talking

smiling   drinking

A 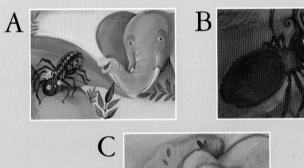 B

C

D 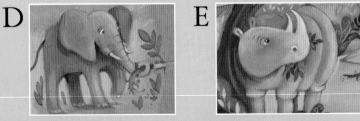 E

Answers to puzzles

Puzzle 1

Puzzle 2

 Anansi was <u>king</u> of the spiders.

 Rhino <u>laughed</u>.

 Anansi tugged the <u>vine</u>.

 Elephant *was* <u>surprised</u>.

A - talking

B - smiling

C - drinking

D - pulling

E - eating

About Anansi

Anansi, the trickster spider, is a popular character in lots of West African and Caribbean folktales. In some stories he appears as a man, or half-man, half-spider.

Designed by Louise Flutter
and Sam Chandler

Series designer: Russell Punter
Digital manipulation: John Russell

First published in 2012 by Usborne Publishing Ltd., Usborne House,
83-85 Saffron Hill, London EC1N 8RT, England. www.usborne.com
Copyright © 2012 Usborne Publishing Ltd.

All rights reserved. No part of this publication may be reproduced,
stored in a retrieval system or transmitted in any form or by any
means, electronic, mechanical, photocopying, recording or otherwise
without the prior permission of the publisher. The name Usborne
and the devices ♀ ⊕ are Trade Marks of Usborne Publishing Ltd.
UE. First published in America in 2012.

USBORNE FIRST READING
Level Two

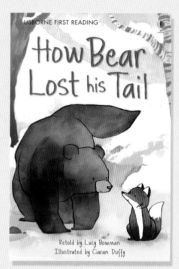

How Bear Lost his Tail

Retold by Lucy Bowman
Illustrated by Ciaran Duffy

Little Miss Muffet

Retold by Russell Punter
Illustrated by Lorena Alvarez

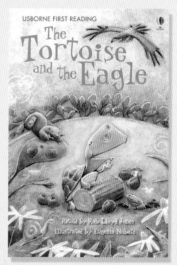

The Tortoise and the Eagle

Retold by Rob Lloyd Jones
Illustrated by Eugenia Nobati

The Genie in the Bottle

Retold by Rosie Dickins
Illustrated by Sara Rojo